SEASON SONG

by MARCY BARACK
pictures by THIERRY COURTIN

 HarperFestival®
A Division of HarperCollinsPublishers

Mud, sand, leaves, snow,
Sing of seasons as we grow.

Sing of spring and slosh in mud,
Pull apart a flower bud,
Meet a robin, hang a screen,
Grab the grass and smell the green.

Pet a kitten, watch the rain
Dripping down the windowpane.
Spring is when we dig and hoe,
Planting veggies in a row.

Sing of summer, sprinkle sand,
Pass a june bug hand to hand,

Steer a sailboat, touch the sea,
Listen to a bumblebee.

Pick a berry, romp in shade,
Pucker up at lemonade.
Summer's when we jump and run,
Chasing bubbles in the sun.

Sing of autumn, roll in leaves,
Tangle with our sweater sleeves,
Hug a pumpkin, climb a stool,
Wave the big kids off to school.

Bury bulbs and trace the frost,
Search for building blocks we lost.
Autumn's when we trick or treat
Covered by a big white sheet.

Sing of winter, stomp in snow,
Catch a cold and have to blow,
Suck on ice and ride a sled,
Feed the blue jays crumbs of bread.

Hang our jackets on a hook,
Play piano, read a book.
Winter's when we stop to stare
At snowflakes drifting in the air.

Sing of seasons as we grow,
Mud, sand, leaves, snow.